SPY
ACADEMY

Mission
Twinpossible

W9-CPE-542

Hugh Ryan

SCHOLASTIC INC.

New York   Toronto   London   Auckland
Sydney   Mexico City   New Delhi   Hong Kong

To my family, who has always supported my dreams of being a ~~spy~~—writer.
—H.R.

ISBN 978-0-545-37173-5

12 11 10 9 8 7 6 5 4 3 2   12 13 14 15 16 17/0

Printed in the U.S.A.   40
First Scholastic printing, January 2012

CHAPTER ONE

Prepare to enter the most dangerous room at Spy Academy," whispered thirteen-year-old Kim Cohen to her twin brother, Ken. She took a deep breath, pulled her dark brown hair into a quick ponytail, and squared her shoulders, getting ready for what was to come.

"I've got your back," said Ken in his deepest, manliest voice. "Let's do it."

St. Perfidious Yearling Academy was the most elite private school in the country, where exceptional children went to learn exceptional skills, to save the world from exceptional dangers.

St. Perfidious graduates had prevented the Instant Message Gang from destroying the Empire State Building, rescued the president from the hands of evil Professor Manimal, and even stopped the Doomsday Ray from obliterating Atlanta.

What, you've never heard of any of these near-disasters?

Well, that's how good Spy Academy is.

Before she could lose her nerve, Kim pushed open the double doors in front of her. A wave of noise washed over them. The school's powerful sonic soundproofing—which Kim had helped build last year—had hidden the noise of the chaos within. Everywhere, people were running wild—throwing things, shooting at one another, eating burritos, setting off traps. Above it all flew dozens of remote-controlled spy robots and satellites. Before Ken and Kim had even stepped through the doors, an electric blue plane with six wings dive-bombed them.

"Duck!" yelled Ken. He pushed Kim out of the way and leaped up, neatly snatching the plane out of the air.

"Ow!" said Kim. "Be careful!"

"Sorry, dude," Ken replied. "But look what I got!"

Ken held the plane up in both hands and prepared to smash it on his knee. It buzzed angrily, trying to get away.

"Wait!" yelled Kim. "Give it to me."

Ken handed the plane to her with a frown. Kim pulled a tiny screwdriver from her pocket, flipped the plane over, and opened it up. She futzed around inside it for a few seconds. When she let go, the plane flew straight up in the air and began to circle the twins.

"That should give us a little protection," said Kim proudly. "We should move before we attract any more attention."

Together, they snuck deeper into the most dangerous room at St. Perfidious: the cafeteria. It was the only place where all the students, regardless of age, grade, or specialization, hung out at the same time. Like every school cafeteria, it was a war zone. But this one was filled with nearly two hundred of the most talented and dangerous kids in the world.

Principal Cornelius Booker recruited each student personally. Even their families didn't know the school's true nature. Kim and Ken's parents thought they were going to a special prep school for extraordinarily gifted children, and while this was true, they were unaware that those gifts included lock picking, computer hacking, and jujitsu.

In the year and a half that Kim and Ken had already spent at Spy Academy, they had learned from the best and brightest spies in the country. From Ippon Sensei, a quiet, middle-aged Japanese woman who had won every fight she'd ever been in, they learned martial arts and physical combat. The mysterious M. Masque—who never looked the same twice—taught them Disguise. Their technology expert was Dr. O, who could hack into any computer in the time it took most people to find the power button. Stealth was taught by Agent 4, a bubbly young woman who dressed like a beauty queen and disappeared like a chameleon. Overseeing them all, and teaching Strategy, was Principal Booker.

None of the teachers was in the cafeteria at the

moment, which was part of the reason it was even crazier than usual. This week was Spy Academy midterms, and the teachers were busy preparing the hardest tests their students would ever take. The students, for their part, were busy studying. Only at Spy Academy, it was hard to tell the difference between a study session and an action movie.

Luckily, the twins were able to secure a table and a few slices of pizza without too much mayhem. They had just started to eat when a high-pitched whine erupted over them.

"Heads up!" called out a voice from above Kim and Ken's table. "Or rather—down!"

A whirling ball the size of a small girl came flying down from the ceiling toward them. It halted just a few inches short of their lunch trays. After three quick spins, it came to a sudden stop and revealed itself to be LaSharah Smith dangling from a rope. LaSharah was Ken's best friend—after Kim, of course.

"Hey, dude, nice moves!" Ken gave LaSharah a high five, sending her into a slight spin. "Getting ready for Sensei's exam, eh?"

"Yup!" LaSharah's dark skin crinkled into a bright smile. "I'm going to wipe the floor with you!"

"Dude, I could bench-press you. In fact, I think I will during the test. Right after I deal with this stupid Tech exam."

"Bring it!"

"Barbarians," mumbled Kim. Her head was bent over her WATCH—Wearable Apparatus for Tracking, Cracking, and Hacking. A WATCH was issued to every student at Spy Academy on the first day of classes. It served as a personal organizer, walkie-talkie, MP3 player, GPS navigator, calculator, and portable gaming system. And in the hands of the Wiz-Kids (as the Tech-focused students like Kim were called), it was also one of the most powerful computer-hacking devices ever made.

LaSharah rolled her eyes. She cocked her fingers and pretended to shoot Ken in the chest, then pressed a button on her harness and flew back up into the cafeteria's rafters.

"Nice one, sis," said Ken. "Life of the party, as usual."

"Sorry, but some of us actually want to study for our exams, you know."

She bit into her pizza without looking up from her WATCH.

"Don't your eyes start to hurt from staring at that thing?" said Ken. "Ugh, Tech class is so boring. I can't wait until I don't have to take it anymore!"

That got Kim's attention. She looked up from her WATCH.

"What?!" she said. "Don't tell me you're going to specialize in Martial Arts."

"Duh," said Ken. He pulled an orange from his pocket and tossed it in the air. With his other hand, he whipped his pocketknife back and forth too fast for Kim's eye to follow. The orange was perfectly peeled and sectioned before it landed on his plate. "Ippon Sensei is awesome, and everyone knows a good spy has to be ready to fight at a moment's notice. But don't worry—I'll let you build me an awesome car or something."

Kim stared at her brother for a moment, then returned to looking at her WATCH. She tapped on a few keys and secretly turned the dial to face her brother.

"What a waste," she said, after a few seconds. "You actually have a brain. Even if you don't like to use it. And for your information, a good spy with the right tech doesn't even need to get near their target to get all the information they need. The closest I plan on coming to a fight is when I send in a robot to rescue you."

"Rescue me?" Ken stood up. "You always think you're sooooo much better than everyone else. You and your 'Wiz-Kid' friends who never leave the labs! Do you want to spend the rest of your life in some dark basement somewhere, building toys for missions you'll never go on?"

"I'd rather do that than spend my time trying to impress everyone with how big my muscles are!"

Ken went red in the face and started sputtering, but Kim ignored him. She played with her WATCH for another minute, while Ken yelled. Then she smiled and held up one finger. The sound of the academy's loudspeaker coming to life cut Ken off.

"Shhh . . ." said Kim. "You're going to want to hear this."

The cafeteria settled down to just a dull roar as students turned their ears to the speakers. Ken's voice suddenly filled the cafeteria.

"You always think you're sooooo much better than everyone else. You and your 'Wiz-Kid' friends who never leave the labs."

Ken stared at Kim.

"Don't worry," Kim said. "I'm broadcasting this in the teachers' lounge as well. Good luck on your Tech midterm with Dr. O."

All around the room, students were pointing at Ken and laughing . . . except for the Wiz-Kids, who were angrily tapping away at their WATCHes. Before his voice had finished echoing in the cafeteria, a dozen remote-controlled spy planes were taking turns diving at him. Kim had disabled their own protection plane, leaving him defenseless.

Ken ducked and twisted and weaved, plucking the planes out of the air and tossing them aside. But even he wasn't fast enough to avoid them all. While he was busy wrestling with a robot that looked like a squid wearing a propeller beanie on top, a bomber opened its doors above his head and covered him in sticky, multicolored glitter.

Ken squinted his eyes at his sister. She pretended not to notice, but he could tell from the way she shifted in her seat that Kim was nervous.

This was going to be fun.

Ken started to walk away, keeping a watch on Kim out of the side of his eye. Just as she decided she was safe and settled down into her chair, he reached out and picked up a spray bottle of whipped cream off one of the cafeteria tables. Kim jumped out of her chair . . . but Ken did nothing except bend down and slowly remove his shoes, which he proceeded to tie together by the laces. Kim sat down again.

The whole cafeteria was still staring at him, but the mood had shifted from laughter to curiosity. What was he up to?

Facing away from Kim, Ken suddenly threw the whipped cream as hard as he could against the wall. The can bounced off the wall, flew over his head, and ricocheted off the ceiling. Without turning around, Ken swung the shoes in a circle over his head and let them fly.

There was the dull sound of shoe leather striking metal, then a loud squirt, then a scream and a clang. Ken turned around to find the whipped cream can on the floor with his shoes wrapped around it. Standing next to it was his sister, who was covered in whipped cream from head to toe.

A bell went off, announcing the end of lunch and the beginning of the next set of tests.

"Good luck in your Physical midterm," Ken called to Kim as he walked out the door. Kim, her mouth too full of whipped cream to speak, sputtered angrily.

CHAPTER TWO

No way!" Ken and Kim yelled simultaneously. Each jumped at the sound of the other's voice.

They were standing back-to-back in a busy hallway, and neither had noticed the other was there. Instead, they had been concentrating on the posted results from yesterday's midterms. They each had just barely passed.

They whirled around to face each other.

"This is your fault!" Again, the twins spoke at the same time. This happened a lot when they were upset . . . and usually made them more upset.

"Stop it!" they yelled.

Other students were beginning to laugh at the two of them speaking in unison. That made the situation even worse. Neither twin said anything for a few seconds. They just stared angrily at each other. Finally, Ken spoke.

"For the midterm, Dr. O made me hack into the school's network and delete the file you posted of me yelling. It was impossible! You ruined my GPA."

"*I* ruined *your* GPA? Do you know how hard it is to pass a wrestling test when you're covered in whipped cream?! I couldn't even grab my opponent, let alone put her in a headlock!"

The twins stared each other down. Around them, other students jostled to read their test results. But before either Ken or Kim could say another word, they suddenly realized they were each holding a pink envelope.

"Did you put this in my hand?" Kim asked Ken.

Ken shook his head no.

"There's only one person who could have slipped these cards into our hands without us noticing. . . ." he said.

"Agent 4!" they said together. This could mean only one thing: the start of their combined Stealth and Disguise midterm. Since it was two midterms in one, this exam was going to be twice as hard as any other.

Kim and Ken tore open the pink envelopes. Inside were scented, handwritten cards that looked like fancy birthday invitations. In bubbly script, they read:

You are cordially invited . . .

to the combined Stealth & Disguise midterm. In the St. Perfidious teachers' lounge there is a locked safe containing important documents. You have one day to devise a plan to retrieve these documents. Tomorrow, starting at exactly the time listed on the back of this card, you will have a one-hour window to execute your plan. Be as stealthy as possible and leave no trace behind. If you do not complete the mission in the time allotted, you fail.

Cordially yours,
Agent 4 & M. Masque

Ken flipped his card over. "One p.m.!" he said. Kim looked at hers.

"Ha! Noon," she said. "Even an extra hour won't help you. I'm going to beat you so bad!"

"You, beat me? Not likely, sis."

"Want to make a bet on it?" Kim stuck out her pinkie. Ken hesitated. Kim was his sister, and sometimes they didn't get along . . . but she was a great spy. And not the kind to take a bet she didn't think she would win.

"Scared?" Kim teased.

Ken grabbed her pinkie with his.

"If I win, you do my laundry for the rest of the semester!" he said. The worst part about specializing in Martial Arts, hands down, was how terrible your gym clothes smelled. And Ippon Sensei wouldn't let students fight if their clothes weren't perfectly laundered.

"Fine," replied Kim. "*When* I win, you'll clean my room."

Kim's room was legendary at St. Perfidious for being the messiest room on campus. She had more bits and pieces of computers, robots, and engineering projects than any dozen other students combined. There was a rumor that a freshman had entered her room looking for a power cord, and had never been seen again.

"Deal!" they said together. And with that, they went their separate ways, each scheming a scheme to ensure that they got the highest grade in the class.

Kim headed straight to the Tech lab, which was hidden in the basement of the school. Well, technically, the whole school was in the basement. To keep parents and neighbors from getting suspicious, there was a typical-looking prep school campus above the real Spy Academy. But if you entered the bathroom on the fourth floor of the East Wing and flushed the second-to-last toilet three times in a row, a secret elevator door opened, granting access to the giant underground complex that was the real school.

The Tech lab was hidden away on the lowest level of the compound, because things in the lab had a tendency to blow up. Not in particularly dangerous ways (well, not usually), but the noises often disturbed the other students. As Kim made her way down three flights of steps, Ken's voice lingered in her ears. He was right. It *was* a dark basement. But Kim loved it down here. And who cared what he thought? He was going to focus on Martial Arts. Martial Arts were for people too dumb to come up with a real plan.

"Kim Cohen."

Kim said her name into the speech recognition box on the outside of the Tech lab. A red glow lit her face, and she knew somewhere a computer was matching a retinal scan to the image of her eye stored in the school's records.

"Welcome, Kim," a robotic voice said as the door slid open.

"Hey, Dr. O," Kim called out as she sat down at her usual worktable and powered up the six computers that she had designed and built by hand as part of her final exam last year. From where she sat, she couldn't see Dr. O, but he almost never left the lab, so she knew he had to be around somewhere.

"What?! Oh, hello there, Kim," Dr. O's slightly

accented English echoed from the other side of the room. He slid out from underneath a half-built robot that he'd been working on all year. No one knew quite what it did yet, perhaps not even Dr. O. But there was no doubt that when it was done, it would be amazing. Dr. O was a certified genius. He had a certificate to prove it. It hung on the wall by the coffeemaker he had invented, which monitored his blood-caffeine level to know when to make a cup of coffee for him.

Kim put on her sweetest voice and asked, "Can you give me the blueprints for the school's security system?"

Dr. O smiled. "Working on the Stealth and Disguise midterm, are we? You know I can't help you."

"Can't blame me for trying. I'll find them anyway."

"And that is why you are my favorite student." Dr. O chuckled. "Now get to work!"

It took Kim three hours to find the layout of the school's security system. But she was in luck. As she had hoped, the teachers' lounge had a security camera installed inside it. Now came the hard part.

Seven hours and fifteen cans of soda later, Kim managed to crack into the school's security system. She was fairly certain she was the first student to ever do so. She trained the security camera in the teachers' lounge on the safe. Now all she had to do was wait until the next time the safe was opened, zoom in, and take some still images of the documents in question. She'd finished the exam before her hour even started, and without leaving a trace behind!

Ken, for his part, went directly to his room and fell asleep. The most important part of his plan was being well rested. When one p.m. rolled around, he walked directly to the teachers' lounge. There, he removed a slim hammer from his pocket, and carefully tapped the door in a few precise places: right over each hinge, and below the knob. Then he took careful aim, lowered his shoulder, and rammed straight into the door. It crumpled like paper—one of the many tricks

Ippon Sensei had taught her favorite student.

Alarms went off. The security camera turned to face the door, but Ken disarmed it with a quick throw of a tennis ball, which bounced off the camera, shattered its lens, and landed right back in his hand. He walked over to the safe, bent at the knees, took a deep breath, and lifted it high over his head. Then he walked out. Three minutes later, he was back in his room.

"Piece of cake," he said to himself.

He considered the rack of tools that hung by his bed. The katana sword wouldn't work. Neither would the sledgehammer. Finally, he settled on a blowtorch and a hacksaw. Ten minutes later, he had the pages in hand.

He knew Kim would call his plan stupid, but it had worked, hadn't it? Simple ideas could be great, regardless of what she thought.

The next morning, the twins woke up early and went to check their grades, each excited to show the other up.

"Scores aren't posted yet," said Ken, who was

already waiting in the hallway when Kim showed up. He was bouncing a tennis ball off the walls and catching it with his eyes closed—something he did when he was bored.

"That's all right," she said. "You can clean my room in the afternoon."

She looked at her WATCH and started reading some of her favorite blogs, her usual way to waste time.

"Ahem."

Ken and Kim both looked up at the sound of a throat clearing. Standing in the hall with them was an old man in a janitor's outfit. He pulled a piece of paper from his pocket and slowly unfolded it.

It was the grades!

Ken and Kim moved out of the way. The janitor slowly walked to the wall. He paused for a second, then removed a roll of tape from his pocket. Painstakingly, he taped the paper to the wall and shuffled away. Ken and Kim leaped forward, searching for their names. After a few seconds, the janitor spoke.

"You're not there," he said in a familiar voice. It was M. Masque in one of his amazing disguises! He was so good, no one knew what he really looked like. Rumor had it even his parents couldn't recognize him.

"What?!" said Ken.

"Why not?!" said Kim.

"Because you both failed. Ms. Cohen, the assignment was to get the documents, not photos of them. What if the critical information had been the fingerprints of someone who had touched them, or something hidden on the back? You have to learn to follow instructions. Not everything can be done from a computer."

"Ha!" laughed Ken.

"And you, Mr. Cohen. This exam was in Stealth and Disguise. You may have taken the evidence with you, but your approach was far from secretive. In the real world, you would have put yourself in grave danger. You may be strong, but strength isn't always the answer."

"Does . . . does this mean we're going to be kicked out?" Kim whispered. She couldn't imagine life without Spy Academy.

"No," said M. Masque, as he shuffled down the hallway. "You're not getting out of this that easily! Agent 4 and I are devising a special extra-credit assignment. Meet us at the helicopter pad tomorrow morning at seven a.m. sharp."

And with that, he turned the corner and disappeared, leaving Ken and Kim alone to contemplate the mysterious assignment that lay before them.

CHAPTER THREE

All night long, Kim and Ken dreamed about their mysterious assignment. If they were meeting at the helipad, their assignment was probably off campus! Students rarely received missions that took them beyond the school until they were upperclassmen. This was going to be the best punishment ever! Would the mission be dangerous? Would they have to infiltrate the grounds of Spy Academy's arch nemesis, the ROGUE (Receivers of a Genuinely Unsavory Education) School? ROGUE students were said to be some of the baddest, most dangerous kids in the world. Of course, they hadn't met Kim and Ken yet! It was more exciting than the first night of Hanukkah.

Sadly, the actual assignment was nowhere near as awesome as their dreams about it were. It was rather like getting a sweater inside the box for a new computer.

"Mr. and Ms. Cohen," began M. Masque, who this morning was dressed as a baby, inside a carriage pushed by Agent 4. "We were sorely disappointed with your performance on yesterday's examination."

Ken couldn't help but wonder how M. Masque had made himself so small! He peeked under the carriage, but there was no sign of the rest of him. His disguise was so good, it was hard to concentrate on what he was saying.

"But we know you have it in you to be great spies!" added Agent 4. "So today, we will be sending you out of St. Perfidious."

Kim tried to contain her excitement, but couldn't. She was bouncing on her toes. Their first real assignment! So what if it was kind of a punishment, and she had to share it with her brother? This was going to be awesome.

"This is Ichabod Saldaña, or Ick for short."

A hologram was projected from the bonnet of the stroller. It showed a young, pale man with long black hair, who was wearing glasses that looked to literally be made out of soda bottles.

"He is a former St. Perfidious student, currently on a long-term independent mission in his own secret laboratory. It's been three weeks since he has checked in with the academy, and Principal Cornelius has become worried."

It must be ROGUE agents! thought Ken with excitement. The idea must have shown on his face, because Agent 4 quickly cut in.

"Now, don't get too excited. Ick is known for this sort of behavior. In fact, this lab assignment was only supposed to be a three-week internship, but he forgot to return . . . for four years. He missed his own graduation."

"Yes," added M. Masque, shaking a baby rattle absentmindedly in his left hand. "This has happened many times before. Which is why we need the two of you to go and remind him to report back to headquarters."

The hologram morphed into a large glass-and-concrete compound. *That,* Kim thought, *must be Ick's secret laboratory.* It was huge! Their mission sounded kind of boring, but at least she'd get to see inside his lab.

"This is Newtown Valley Mall," said Agent 4. "It has over two hundred thousand square feet of stores, plazas, food courts, and entertainment, including a bowling alley and two movie theaters!"

The main doors of the mall opened, and the hologram dissolved in a swirl. When it re-formed, it showed the entrance to an upscale maternity clothes boutique named Bun in the Oven.

"Inside dressing room number three is the secret entrance to Ick's lab. My disguise today is in honor of his creativity in choosing this hiding place," said M. Masque.

"For three years, Ick has used his stealth and disguise skills to sneak all kinds of technology in and out of this store, without ever being detected," added Agent 4. She gently rocked the carriage back and forth, making the hologram waver in the air. "You two will follow his example. This mission may not be dangerous, but a good spy goes undetected at all times. You must not compromise Ick's laboratory. You will be required to—what's that saying?—'hide in plain sight.' Good luck."

Personally, Kim thought it was a lot easier to hide in hidden sight than to hide in plain sight, but this was the assignment.

A beat-up blue minivan pulled up in front of the helipad. Ken turned to ask Agent 4 a question, but she and M. Masque were nowhere to be found. It was a little creepy the way they did that so quickly and so quietly.

"I guess this is our ride," said Kim. She was disappointed that there was no helicopter. In fact, the whole mission was a little disappointing. But she was still determined to do better on it than Ken . . . just as soon as she could figure out what that would mean.

Inside the minivan, a gray glass barrier separated the driver from the backseat where Kim and

Ken sat. Try as they might, they couldn't make out the face of the person in the front seat.

A blueprint of the mall was sitting on the seat next to them, and they studied it carefully during the drive. Both wanted to talk about the mission, but they were still angry at each other, and neither wanted to be the first one to speak. So instead they sat silently the entire way to the Newtown Valley Mall. It was a long ride.

CHAPTER FOUR

The minivan let them out in the mall parking lot, which was a vast asphalt sea filled with other minivans nearly identical to their own. The front window rolled down, revealing their mysterious driver.

"Bye, kids!" yelled Agent 4. "Now, be good, and I'll be back to pick you up right here at three p.m." She waved good-bye, rolled up the window, and drove off. Anyone watching would have thought she was Ken and Kim's mother. When it came to hiding in plain sight, no one could top Agent 4.

"How did she get from being right in front of us

to being inside that van?" wondered Kim aloud as she watched Agent 4 drive off. Ken shrugged. The teachers at Spy Academy were just that good.

Kim pulled the blueprint of the mall from her pocket and looked at it again. Ken peered over her shoulder.

"Here's what I think we should do," said Ken. "First, we knock out the security guard here." He pointed to one of the many entrances to the behind-the-scenes maintenance areas of the mall. "Then we get into the ventilation system, and head toward Ick's lab that way."

"Yeah, that's a great plan," said Kim with a laugh. "Didn't you learn anything from failing the exam? We can't just go knocking people out. We have to be stealthy."

She paused, and Ken grabbed the map out of her hands.

"So you mean we should act like normal kids?" he said sarcastically. "You know, the kind that don't study blueprints in parking lots?"

"I don't need the blueprints." Kim laughed. "A place like this? The security system is about as tough as Velcro. Once I hack in, we wait until the mall closes, disable the cameras, open the doors remotely, and walk right into Ick's lab."

Kim sat down on the curb and started tapping on her WATCH, getting right to it.

"Great plan," said Ken with fake enthusiasm. "But Agent 4 said she'd be back at three p.m., remember? We don't have time to wait."

Kim stopped typing. She hated to admit it, but Ken was right.

"Let's just go see what the place looks like," the twins said in unison.

Pointedly not speaking to each other, Ken and Kim stomped their way to the mall. When they were angry, they looked the most alike. Both walked quickly, with their eyes squinted, their brows furrowed, and their arms swinging rapidly. A clown was handing out balloons at the entrance to the mall, but she took one look at Ken and Kim and walked off in the other direction.

The shopping center was one of those fancy malls, where the floors were marble and there were statues at all of the intersections. Big stone flowerpots and uncomfortable-looking benches were set throughout the hallways. All three floors of the mall were busy, but not too crowded.

Ken and Kim tried their best to blend in, but they were too obviously still angry at each other. As they walked through the mall, everyone got out of their way. Bun in the Oven was on the second floor, near the very center of the mall. When they got close, they paused.

"Let's sit there," Ken suggested, pointing to a bench with a good view of the store.

Kim plopped down on the bench and pulled out a book. She pretended to read while she surveyed the scene.

"Looks like there's just the one store clerk," she said. "Early fifties, gray hair, over by the cash register. No customers."

"That means fewer people to avoid, but also fewer people to use as cover," said Ken, who was pretending to tie his shoe. "And that saleslady is watching the door to the store very carefully. She must be bored out of her mind and just hoping someone comes in."

"I can't see any other entrance," said Kim. She thought about their options. "We're going to have to follow Agent 4's example: Hide in plain sight. We'll just walk right in and take a look at the dressing rooms."

"What will we tell the saleslady when she comes to talk to us?" said Ken. "'Hi, we're pregnant'?"

"We'll say we're looking for our mother," Kim responded. "Kids get separated from their parents at the mall all the time."

Kim stood up and headed toward the store. Ken followed a few feet behind her. The store was filled with every kind of maternity clothing Kim could imagine, and some she couldn't. *What is a maternity headband?* she wondered. *And how is it any different from a regular headband?*

The second they stepped into Bun in the Oven, the salesclerk was suddenly right next to them. For an old woman, she sure could move fast! Maybe it was just that they were on a mission, but something about the salesclerk gave Ken the creeps.

"Can I help you?" she asked. Ken could tell right away that she was one of those people who pretended to like kids, but really didn't. Her name tag read MS. SIDAL.

Ken put on his best fake smile (one of the first lessons they learned from Agent 4), and turned to her.

"Hi!" he said. "We're looking for our mother. Have you seen her?"

Ken stepped in front of the saleswoman, hiding Kim from her view. Out of the corner of his eye, he saw Kim sneak past her. Without discussing it, they knew exactly how to handle this situation. He would keep the woman busy, while Kim checked out the store. Ken had forgotten what a good team they made.

"No," said Ms. Sidal. "I'm the onl—"

But Ken cut her off before she could finish.

"My mom looks kind of like me, but with longer hair. And she's, like, *this* tall."

Ken swung his arm to show her height, and knocked over a display of special maternity socks.

"Oh no! I'm so sorry," Ken sputtered. Of course, he had done it on purpose. "Let me pick these up."

He bent down to pick up the socks, and

accidentally knocked into the saleslady, who almost fell down on top of him.

"Ugh!" she yelled. "You clumsy idiot!"

"I'm sorry," said Ken. He picked up a big handful of socks—too many, in fact, and they all fell again as he tried to put them back in place. "Oh gosh!"

"Stop!" Ms. Sidal yelled. "I'll get them. Wait— where did your sister go?"

She jumped up and scanned the store. Luckily, Kim was just behind her.

"Here," said Kim, holding out a stray sock. "Some of these flew pretty far. Geez, Ken. Could you get more klutzy? Anyway. Mom's not here. We should go."

"Thanks for your help, ma'am," said Ken, as they exited the store.

The twins walked a little way down the hall. They stopped in front of one of the mall computer terminals, which had maps and directories of all the stores. While Kim pretended to search for the location of GameWOW, a fancy computer and electronics store, they compared notes.

"Anything?" Ken whispered.

"No. The changing room had an out-of-order sign on it. How can a changing room be out of order? Is the mirror broken?"

The hair on the back of Ken's neck went up. What if something really was wrong with Ick?

"That salesclerk was really aggressive," he said. "You don't think she knows something is up, do you?"

Kim hesitated. "No?" she said finally. But she didn't sound certain.

"Maybe we should call the academy and check in," said Ken. "If there is a real problem, they'd want to know. We're not full agents yet."

Reluctantly, Kim agreed. She didn't want to fail the exam—again—but if another agent was in real danger, that went way beyond a training mission. Kim set her WATCH to cell mode and called M. Masque, while Ken made sure no one was listening.

"'Allo, 'allo, 'allo." A British woman answered the phone. "Bits 'n' Bobs Thrift Store. 'Alf off on Thursdays!"

"Agents Cohen and Cohen, checking in," Kim responded. "Code is Bravo Niner Sierra Alpha." Every student at Spy Academy had two phone codes: one to give if they were safe, and one to give if it was an emergency and they were in danger. Kim used her safe code.

"Agents Cohen. I trust there haven't been any problems," said M. Masque, dropping the British accent. He didn't sound pleased to hear from them already.

"Well, no, not exactly." Kim squirmed. "It's just—well, we got to the store, and the salesclerk was strange, and there's an out-of-order sign on the dressing room, and we were worried."

It sounded stupid when she said it out loud. She wished Ken had been the one to make the call.

"This is exactly the sort of real-world problem a good spy must be ready to deal with," M. Masque said, sounding frustrated. "Unless the two of you are giving up on your mission?"

"No, no!" yelled Kim. "We're totally on it. We were just keeping you in the loop."

"Good, then," replied M. Masque. "Carry on.

Agent 4 and I will see you at three p.m."

With that, he hung up.

"Now what?" said Kim.

"Dude, I still think something is weird about that saleslady," said Ken.

"Agreed," said Kim. "But until we have proof, we can't call back. They'll fail us!"

The last thing Kim wanted was to leave Spy Academy. It was the only school she'd ever loved!

"How about this," she said. "Let's get some more information. If anything else seems really strange, we call Monsieur Masque and tell him we think something is wrong."

Ken thought it over. He didn't want to return to normal school, either. He stuck out his hand.

"Deal," he said.

They shook hands and smiled at each other.

Kim looked at the computer terminal they were standing in front of.

"I've got an idea," she said.

CHAPTER FIVE

Let's see if we can find out anything more about that aggressive saleslady," said Kim, as her fingers flew across the keyboard of the computer terminal.

"What are you doing?" asked Ken. Idly, he threw a SuperBall against the side of the terminal. It flew up, bounced off one of the lights on the ceiling, and landed perfectly back in his hand.

"This is a local access network. It's like a mini-Internet, but just for the computers in this mall," Kim explained. "Give me a minute, and I should be able to get all the staff information from Bun in the Oven."

A few seconds passed. Kim typed so fast it sounded like tiny machine-gun fire. Blue and red lights flickered across the screen. A window popped up, asking for a password, but Kim ignored it. She typed in a few more words. Suddenly, the mall map dissolved, and a new screen appeared.

"Here we go," she said. Dozens of stores were listed on the screen. But no Bun in the Oven.

"Their computers aren't on the network," said Kim.

"That's suspicious," said Ken. "Should we call Monsieur Masque?"

"No way," said Kim. "There could be lots of reasons why they aren't on the network. Their computers might be really old, or their connection might be down, or anything."

"True. Or that saleslady could be a ROGUE agent and Ick could be in a world of danger," said Ken.

"She's too old to be a ROGUE student," said Kim. Then a terrible thought crossed her mind. "But she could be one of their professors."

If the ROGUE professors were anywhere near

as good as the teachers at St. Perfidious, that would make that old lady one of the most dangerous people on the planet! That wasn't possible . . . *was it?*

"Is there another way you can get into her computer?" asked Ken.

Kim thought about it. She was about to say something when Ken interrupted her.

"Come on," he said. "Let's get to that GameWOW. I want to see if they have the new Zombie Killer IV yet!"

"What?" said Kim. Right then, a hand tapped her on the shoulder.

"Excuse me," said an older man in a distinguished-looking suit. "Are you kids still using this?"

"Oh!" said Kim. For a minute, she'd forgotten that they were in the middle of the mall, and that they were supposed to be acting like normal teenagers. "No, it's all yours. Come on, Ken, let's go get Zombie Killer . . . uhhh . . . IV?"

While she spoke, Kim typed quickly on the terminal's keyboard, bringing the regular map back up and undoing all of the work she had just done.

The twins walked quickly away from the computer terminal. Ken led the way down the crowded mall hallway. There were so many people bustling about, it was hard to find a moment to talk. Finally, they found a quiet spot by an empty storefront.

"Good save back there," said Kim.

"Thanks," said Ken. "I guess I'm learning this stealth stuff . . . slowly."

"There is one other way into the computer," said Kim.

She fiddled with her WATCH. Carefully, she pulled a small silver button off its side.

"This is a PARASITE," she said. "It stands for Personal Access Retrieval . . ."

Kim paused and thought.

"Personal Account Resignation?" she tried again. "No, that's not it. Partial Armadillo Reiteration? Argh!"

Kim stamped her foot in frustration. "I can never remember what it stands for. But it will allow me to access all the files on that computer. But the tricky part is this: It has to be sitting right on the computer to work. There is no way that nosy saleslady will let us put this on her computer."

"Let me see it," said Ken.

Kim handed the PARASITE to him. Ken weighed it in his hand. He tossed it lightly in the air a few times. He held it up close to his face and inspected it.

"How tough is it?" he asked.

"Pretty much indestructible," said Kim. "You could drive a truck over it."

"Perfect." Ken smiled. "Let me handle this."

The twins headed back to Bun in the Oven, but stopped before they stepped into the saleslady's line of sight. If she really was a ROGUE professor, there was no need to tip her off. They pretended to look at a snack machine while they discussed their plan.

"Here's what we do," said Ken. "This time, you distract her. All I need you to do is make sure her back is to the computer. Think you can handle it?"

"No problem," said Kim. "What are you going to do?"

"Just watch," said Ken, smiling.

Kim walked over to Bun in the Oven. Inside,

the salesclerk was yelling at a woman who was obviously pregnant. Just as Kim walked in the door, the woman came running out crying.

Wow, talk about a terrible sales pitch, thought Kim.

Ms. Sidal stood behind the counter, tapping away at her computer.

"You again?" she said, looking up from her keyboard. "What do you want now? Your mother still isn't here, unless that was her. And if it was, I suggest you go chase her down, because I'm pretty sure she won't be coming back."

Ms. Sidal smiled a nasty smile and adjusted her gray hair, which was done up in a bun with two big chopsticks poked through it.

"No," said Kim, in her best scared-little-girl voice. "It's my brother! I can't find him, either."

"Well, honey, he's not here," said Ms. Sidal, without looking up from the keyboard. "Good luck and good-bye."

"Please," said Kim. "Will you help me look for him?" She tried to make herself cry by thinking about sad things, like dead puppies, but all she could manage were a few sniffles. She still had to work on that trick.

"Sorry, kid. Not my job."

Ms. Sidal refused to budge from the computer. Outside, Kim could see Ken lingering by the bench, waiting. She couldn't let him down.

An idea occurred to her—a way to get Ms. Sidal away from the computer *and* see if she knew anything about Ick's lab.

"Maybe he's hiding in here somewhere," said Kim. "He does that when he's scared."

Kim started walking toward the fitting rooms. Faster than a bolt of lightning, Ms. Sidal was there, standing between Kim and the back of the store.

"I said he's not here," she repeated firmly.

"But, ma'am, please!" Kim said. "I have to find him!"

While Kim and Ms. Sidal argued, Ken stood up and estimated the distance to the computer. Ms. Sidal had eagle eyes and was sure to notice if he walked into the store. But the PARASITE was tiny, and if he threw it just right, she'd never see.

Ken took a deep breath, pulled the PARASITE out of his pocket, and took aim. Then he threw it as hard as he could. It hit the floor right at the entrance to Bun in the Oven. Ms. Sidal's eyes flicked up at the noise, but the PARASITE was below her line of sight, and she went right back to arguing with Kim.

The PARASITE bounced off the floor and flew to the right, hitting the garment rack Ken had knocked over before. It smacked into one of the rack's metal corners, which sent it flying straight up into the air, right into the ceiling fan. The blade of the fan hit it like a baseball bat, and it zoomed toward the sales desk like a home run.

As Ken watched, it plopped down right on top of the computer tower. It bounced and landed at the very edge of the hard drive. It teetered dangerously. Ken held his breath. Miraculously, the PARASITE stayed in place.

"Yes!" Ken said quietly. He pumped his fist in the air. He was a total ninja!

Ken ran into the store. He could hear Kim and the saleswoman arguing.

"I know he's not here!" yelled Ms. Sidal. Then she caught sight of Ken.

"There!" she yelled. "He's right there. Now get out, both of you!"

"Where have you been?" yelled Kim.

"Me?" said Ken. "You're the one who disappeared."

Ken grabbed Kim's hand and pretended to pull her out of the store. He squeezed her hand once. Kim looked him in the eye and quirked her eyebrow. He gave a tiny nod. Kim smiled.

"Mom's got to be here somewhere," she said loudly as they exited the store. "Let's go find her!"

CHAPTER
SIX

Did it work?" Kim whispered to Ken as they left the store.

"Dude, of course it worked," said Ken. "It was a piece of cake."

"Awesome work, bro!" Kim gave Ken a high five.

"We make a pretty good team," said Ken. He sounded only a little bit surprised.

"We should work together more often," said Kim. "Only without the part where we nearly fail out of school first."

"Right," said Ken. "So what now? How do we get the data off the computer?"

"Give me two minutes," said Kim, "and I'll have that hard drive singing like Justin Bieber!"

The twins sat down on the bench outside of Bun in the Oven. Kim fiddled with her WATCH for a minute.

"Hmmm . . ." she said. "They've got better security than the rest of the mall."

"Can you crack it?" asked Ken.

"Um, yeah?" replied Kim. "Do you know who you're talking to? Of course I can."

Despite her brave words, Kim wondered for a moment if she could. The security on Bun in the Oven's computer was nearly as good as Spy Academy's own! There were passwords, multiple clearance checks, and a nasty little virus that tried to destroy her WATCH when she accidentally activated it. It took all the skills that Dr. O had taught her just to stay one step ahead of the computer's artificial intelligence program. But in the end, she pulled it off.

"There!" she said gleefully. "Open for business. Now, let's see what we've got."

Scrolling lists of text began filling up the screen of her WATCH.

"Inventory, boring. Receipts, boring. Here we go! Employee records."

Kim was silent for a second.

"Uh-oh," she said.

"What's up?" asked Ken, trying to peer over her shoulder at the small screen.

"That saleslady isn't on their employee list. See, here are all their photos." Kim pulled up a page of nearly identical smiling young women. "There is no way that salesclerk is one of these girls. Not unless she's been working at Bun in the Oven since '07. Nineteen-oh-seven, that is!"

"Suspicious," Ken agreed.

"According to the logs, the last time a registered Bun in the Oven employee checked in was three days ago—the day Ick's signal stopped transmitting! Which is also the same day the computer's security program was beefed up."

"This is definitely not good," Ken said.

"And someone has been using this computer to

send encrypted e-mails through a router in southern Kyrgyzstan! I'm trying to open one now."

"Kim," Ken said, tugging on her sleeve.

"One second!" replied Kim. "I've almost got the e-mail open."

"Kim!" said Ken more urgently.

"I'm in!" Kim paused for a second while she read the e-mail. "Ken! That salesclerk is Homa Sidal!"

Homa Sidal was the ROGUE School's dean of information. She taught Interrogation Techniques and Advanced Rogueishness. Somehow, Kim doubted that working at Bun in the Oven was something she did for fun.

"They've got Ick!" Kim whispered. "Apparently, he created a working prototype of a sonic disruptor. It's capable of tearing a building in half with pure sound. Homa Sidal has been sent here to make him talk!"

"Kim!" Ken yelled as quietly as he could. "Look."

Kim raised her head from her WATCH. Homa Sidal was staring right at them!

"I think we've been—" Ken started to say, but before he could finish, Homa reached down and pressed a button on the computer keyboard. Even from fifty feet away, Ken and Kim could hear the sound of large locks locking down the dressing rooms.

"—identified," Ken finished. As they watched, a steel panic door descended from the ceiling of the store, cutting off all access to the dressing rooms.

"Time to go!" said Kim. As she stood up, Homa pulled one of the chopsticks from her hair bun. Silver and sharp, it glittered under the fluorescent lights.

"Duck!" yelled Ken, as Homa took aim and whipped the razor-sharp stake through the air. He grabbed Kim by the arm and pulled her to the side.

Thunk!

The stake missed Kim's head by mere inches, and buried itself instead in her forearm!

"Ahhh!" screamed Kim.

"Are you okay?" asked Ken. He could see the quivering shaft of the stake poking out of her arm. It didn't look good.

"No!" said Kim. "She broke my WATCH."

Kim held up her arm. The stake had punctured the very center of her WATCH, like a dart in a bull's-eye. A single spark flew out of the side, and Ken watched as the screen went black. Luckily, Kim's WATCH had stopped the dart from piercing her actual arm.

"You're going to pay for that!" yelled Kim.

Homa reached up to pull the other stake from her hair, and the twins took off running down the hallway.

"Hey! Watch where you're going!" A man carrying three giant bags yelled at Kim. But it was too late for her to slow down. She bumped right into him.

"Sorry!" said Kim. She helped him back to his feet. A good spy was a polite spy.

"Now what?" yelled Ken. Homa's second dart whizzed past him and embedded itself in the plastic mascot of Chick-Chick-Boom!, a local fried chicken chain. At least now she was unarmed . . . hopefully. The twins continued running.

Kim dodged a woman with a baby stroller the

size of a tank, and then ducked under the arms of a couple holding hands. What they needed, she realized, was a distraction that would slow Homa Sidal down, and give them enough time to call Spy Academy. But what?

"There!" Kim yelled, pointing to the side of the hallway where a small glass window covered a red fire alarm lever. Printed on the window in neat letters were the words IN CASE OF EMERGENCY, BREAK GLASS.

This definitely qualifies, thought Kim. The only problem was the two dozen or so people between them and the fire alarm. If Homa caught them, they were in way more trouble than a failed exam.

Ken didn't even slow down. In one fluid motion, he bent his head forward and launched himself at the ground. He rolled quickly through the first cluster of people. As he came up from his roll, he leaped into the air and grabbed onto a low-hanging light, which he used to swing over the heads of the remaining crowd (who were so impressed by his performance, they applauded, thinking he was some sort of entertainment hired by the mall). He landed directly in front of the fire alarm.

Smash! went the glass. Ken reached in and yanked the lever. Instantly, a dozen sirens started going off. The mall was filled with flashing red lights. People poured out of the stores, filling up the hallway and making it impossible for Homa Sidal to reach them. But it wouldn't stop her for long.

"This way!" Kim yelled, pointing down a short side hallway. If she remembered the map right, this would lead them to Bull's-Eye, the giant department store that anchored the mall.

"It's a dead end!" said Ken. "We'll be trapped."

"Trust me," Kim replied. With a shrug, Ken followed her.

The hallway ended at the entrance to Bull's-Eye. Shoppers were streaming out, trying to get to the nearest exit. Kim pushed her way through, and Ken did his best to follow her.

"This way," Kim said, pointing to the center of the store. She led them to an escalator, which took them up to the third floor of the mall. From here, they exited back out into the mall's main hallway.

This floor had fewer stores, and most people had already evacuated thanks to the fire alarm.

"There," said Kim. "Even if she did follow us into the store, she won't know whether we went up or down the escalators. That should buy us some time."

"We've got to call the school!" said Ken. "We need backup, pronto. But your WATCH is broken, and I didn't bring mine because I never know how to use it."

Kim gave Ken a dirty look, and he blushed. "I should learn," he mumbled.

"Well," said Kim, "I hope you've learned an important lesson. It's a good thing you have me here."

She paused.

"Say it," she said.

"I've learned an important lesson and it's a good thing you're here! Now, how are we going to call headquarters?"

Kim pulled a cell phone from her pocket.

"Where did you get that?" Ken asked. Cell phones were strictly forbidden at Spy Academy, lest someone accidentally let confidential information slip over a tapped line.

"Remember that guy I bumped into?"

Ken nodded.

"I took it from his pocket as I helped him up."

"Kim!" said Ken. "That's stealing!" They might be spies, but they weren't thieves.

"It was an emergency!" replied Kim. "Besides, I took this, too, so I'd have his address and we could send it back to him."

She held up the man's wallet.

Before Ken could say anything, Kim put the cell phone to her ear.

"Uh-oh," she said. "I was afraid of this. They're jamming phone reception!"

Kim tried again, but it was no use. The phone wouldn't work.

Ken grabbed her shoulder and took the phone from her hands.

"We don't have time to keep trying," he said. "They know we're here. Homa Sidal is looking for us. ROGUE agents could be moving Ick off-site as we speak. We're on our own. We've got to rescue Ick ourselves."

CHAPTER SEVEN

Okay, what's our first objective?" Kim said.

"To rescue Ick," said Ken.

"Second objective?"

"To keep the sonic disruptor prototype out of ROGUE hands."

"So we need to . . . ?"

The twins considered for a second. They were hidden inside a janitor's closet right by the entrance to the Bull's-Eye department store. They'd needed a place to think where neither mall security nor ROGUE agents would bother them. This was the best they could do. Ken was squatting atop a mop bucket, while Kim leaned against shelves full of cleaning products.

"Well, Ick and the prototype must still be in his lab," said Ken. "Or why else would Homa Sidal be guarding it? So we need to get past that steel panic door."

"She activated the defense system using the store computer. If I can repair my WATCH, I can deactivate it. The mall's GameWOW should have all the parts I need."

Ken pulled out the mall map from his pocket. As luck would have it, GameWOW was also on the third floor. But it was all the way on the other side of the mall. They would have to run down one long hallway, through the mall food court, and then down another hallway—all without getting caught by Homa Sidal.

"Ready?" said Ken, as he prepared to open the door.

"Ready!" said Kim.

Ken opened the door and the twins burst out running. The fire alarm was still going off, and the shrieking sirens and flashing lights made the mall seem scary and strange. The twins hadn't gone more than ten feet before they heard the whirring sound of a camera turning to follow them. ROGUE agents must have taken over the mall security system! The twins' only hope was to outrun them. Thankfully, the first hallway was totally empty.

When they reached the food court, Ken and Kim skidded to a halt. The large circular room was filled with tables and chairs arranged in a ring around a water fountain in the middle. Sitting at one of the large tables was a group of four girls in matching school uniforms: black shoes, white kneesocks, plaid skirts, and gray jackets. They hardly seemed to notice the alarms going off around them.

"Hey," yelled Ken. "Can't you hear the sirens? You've got to get out of here right now!" One of the first rules Spy Academy students learned was to get all civilians out of potential danger areas.

As one, the schoolgirls turned to look at Ken and Kim. As they did, Kim's heart sank. All four wore the faceless ninja masks of ROGUE students!

They were made to hide the ROGUEs' identities and scare their enemies, but personally, Kim thought it made them look like weird plastic dolls.

"Come on, girls!" yelled one of the ROGUE agents. "Let's get 'em!"

The girls exploded to their feet. They moved impossibly fast.

"Stay behind me!" Ken said to Kim. "I'll take care of this."

The girls fanned out as they approached, so that each of them came toward Ken and Kim from a different angle.

"This is going to be fun," said one. She swung a large brown purse back and forth in front of her as she walked. She giggled. "I've always wanted to find out how good you Spy Academy brats really are."

She darted forward, her bag swinging. Ken leaped out to meet her, grabbing one of the mall chairs to use as a shield. The bag hit the chair with a boom like a thunderclap. The chair exploded into pieces. Ken was defenseless.

"That the best you can do?" the girl taunted

Ken. Around them, the other girls laughed and hissed.

Slowly, the girl forced Ken backward with her purse. Suddenly, he tripped over one of the pieces of the broken chair. He stumbled onto one knee, and the ROGUE agent swung her purse in an arc straight at his head.

"Ken!" Kim screamed. "Watch out!"

At the last minute, Ken ducked beneath the girl's swing. He grabbed her arm as it passed and pushed as hard as he could. The weight of her purse combined with the strength of Ken's shove sent her spinning like a top.

"Watch out, you idiot!" yelled one of the other ROGUE agents, as the first girl spun right toward her. But there was nothing she could do to slow herself.

Bam!

The two ROGUE agents slammed into each other.

Splash!

They landed in a sopping heap in the food court fountain. Two down, two to go.

The remaining two schoolgirls screamed and came at Ken simultaneously.

"You'll pay for that," yelled the one on his right. She pulled the earphones from her MP3 player and cracked them like a whip. Even from a distance, Kim could tell these were no ordinary headphones. They must have been made out of impossibly thin, incredibly strong carbon steel microfilaments. Nothing could break them.

The agent on Ken's left removed the barrettes from her hair and held them up like daggers. Kim could see the razor-sharp points on their teeth. Ken was in trouble!

Ken picked up a long wooden piece from the broken chair and charged at the girl with the barrettes.

Snip! Snap!

The barrettes clacked open and shut as the ROGUE agent attacked Ken. But Ken was too fast for her. Every time, her barrettes closed on the empty air where Ken had been just moments before.

Meanwhile, the girl with the whip circled the

two fighters, waiting for the right moment to dive in. Ken watched her out of the corner of his eye. He had to time this just right.

Snip!

Ken dived to the left.

Snap!

Ken jumped to the right.

Any second now, Ken thought to himself. And then it happened. The girl with the whip raised her hand, preparing to snap it around Ken's neck. But the girl with the barrettes attacked him at the same moment! Ken shoved his wooden pole into the sharp mouths of the barrettes, which closed on it and got stuck. Then he jumped backward, stretching the other ROGUE schoolgirl's arms out just as the whip came down right where he had been standing a second before. Fast as a snake, the whip wrapped around the first girl's wrists, neatly tying her up and disarming her partner at the same time. He shoved Barrette Girl into Whip Girl, and they both fell to the ground.

"Run!" yelled Ken. He and Kim took off through the food court. He just hoped he'd bought them enough time to make it to GameWOW.

Kim was two steps behind Ken as they ran. They'd almost made it out of the food court when something flashed through the air between them and hit Ken in the back.

Kim stared in surprise at the small white box with a screen on the front of it. It was Whip Girl's MP3 player, and it was stuck to Ken!

The song title read "Fire Bomb," with a counter underneath it that had thirty seconds on it.

Twenty-nine.

Twenty-eight.

"What is it?" yelled Ken. Still running, he tried to reach around to yank the MP3 player off of him, but it was right between his shoulder blades where he couldn't reach.

"It's nothing!" said Kim. "Keep running."

Nothing but a bomb disguised as an MP3 player! she thought to herself. Luckily, Bomb Squad had been one of her Spy Academy extracurricular activities.

Kim pulled out a pocketknife and popped the cover off the MP3 player, revealing a nest of wires and two very small sticks of dynamite. As bombs went, it was tiny, but still not something you'd want exploding while it was attached to you.

"If it's nothing," said Ken, "what are you doing?"

"Nothing!" replied Kim. "It's fine! Now, quiet. I need to concentrate."

Kim stared at the wires. It was hard to do this while running. But if they stopped, the ROGUE agents would be on them. She was beginning to appreciate all of the physical training Ken did. This would be a lot easier if she wasn't breathing so hard. Ken was lucky she had a steady hand.

Green wire connects to the timer, she thought to herself. *So the red one has to be the detonator. Or is it the blue one? No. It's the red one. Definitely the red one.*

With a flick of her penknife, Kim cut the red wire. To her relief, the countdown stopped. She couldn't get the device off of him—it was stuck with some impossibly strong glue—but at least it was deactivated.

As they left the food court, Kim glanced

quickly behind her. The ROGUE agents were getting to their feet. They'd be back after them in no time.

"We have to hurry!" Kim yelled. "They're right behind us."

But she realized that even if they made it to the store before the ROGUEs caught up with them, there was no way she'd have the time she needed to fix her WATCH. They were done for.

Suddenly Ken stopped.

"Keep going," he yelled at Kim.

He turned to face the oncoming ROGUE agents. Ken was one of the best martial artists Spy Academy had, but he'd been lucky last time. Now that the agents knew what he could do, he doubted that they would come at him one at a time. And even he would be hard-pressed to defeat four ROGUE spies at the same time.

"Ken, you can't do this!" Kim yelled. "There has to be another way." She couldn't let him sacrifice himself! They were a team.

"You're the only one of us who can get that

door open," replied Ken. "I'll buy you the time you need."

Kim looked back at the ROGUE agents running toward them. She hesitated.

"Go!" yelled Ken. "Complete the mission. You're our only hope! Ick needs you. Spy Academy needs you! Now go!"

Kim ran.

CHAPTER
EIGHT

Kim ran to GameWOW at top speed. Behind her, the sound of fighting faded into the distance. Ken was buying her time; she had to make the most of it! But when she finally reached the store, it was closed.

It must have locked automatically when the clerks evacuated because of the alarm, she realized. If her WATCH had been working, she could have hacked into the computers . . . but that was the whole reason she was here in the first place.

She looked through the large glass window at the array of video games and electronics. Everything she needed was in there.

Kim thought for a second. Her usual techie tricks weren't going to work in this situation. What would Ken do in her shoes?

She spotted a large ceramic pot filled with flowers next to a bench a few stores down. She grabbed it. Man, was it heavy! As fast as she could, she ran back to GameWOW.

This isn't going to be subtle, she thought.

Kim lifted the flowerpot above her head and heaved it through the window.

CRASH!

She'd have to make sure that the academy paid the store back for the damage when all this was done, but it worked! She was in GameWOW.

Quickly, Kim ran down the aisles, pulling things off the shelves. A Wi-Fi-enabled smartphone, a retro-classic arcade joystick, four rechargeable lithium batteries, and, finally, the power cord from an old game system. Unfortunately, the only phone that had all the parts she needed was decorated with purple ponies and glittery butterflies, which meant that her WATCH was going to look like a five-year-old girl's birthday party. But at least it would work again.

Kim tore all the packaging apart and put the pieces on the ground, along with her broken WATCH. She pulled Homa Sidal's deadly chop-stick out and set to work. Thankfully, Dr. O made all of the advanced Tech students prove that they could dismantle, repair, and put back together their WATCHes before he allowed them to take the highest-level classes.

Twice, Kim had to stop what she was doing because her hands were shaking so hard. She tried not to think about Ken, and what was happen-ing to him. He hadn't come and found her, but neither had the ROGUEs, so she could only guess that they had taken him captive. Now both he *and* Ick were in ROGUE clutches. She had her work cut out for her. Once her WATCH was repaired, she was certain she could open that steel panic door . . . but then what? At the very least, she'd be facing four ROGUE students and Homa Sidal!

Kim decided she'd worry about things one step at a time. Finally, after what seemed like hours, she'd managed to replace all the broken parts of her WATCH. With her fingers crossed, she held down the power button. . . .

And her WATCH came to life! Despite the butterflies and ponies, it was as good as new.

First, she tried to call Spy Academy. But whatever was jamming cell phone reception was also blocking her WATCH's calls. If she had enough time, she knew she'd be able to get through the jammer, but the ROGUE agents would be gone by that point. She needed to act fast.

Quickly, she used her WATCH and the GameWOW store computer to access the mall's security system. It took her only a minute to break through the passwords and protections that the ROGUE hackers had put on when they took over the mall cameras.

Hmph, she thought to herself. *ROGUE students aren't* that *impressive when it comes to computer security.*

Kim began pulling up the security camera feeds on her WATCH. The first few showed nothing out of the ordinary, just closed stores and empty hallways. But on the fifth, she struck gold. The four ROGUE agents were dragging a tied-up

Ken behind them. One of the agents was limping, and another had a big black eye.

At least Ken went down fighting, Kim thought.

With a few more clicks, she pulled up the sound on the computer. Now she could hear the girls talking.

"So how does it feel knowing your partner abandoned you?" one of the girls taunted Ken.

"She must be such a coward," said another.

Kim's blood started to boil. A coward, huh? She'd show them.

"Shut up!" yelled Ken. "You watch—she's twice the spy all of you combined will ever be!"

"What, did she run off to get your babysitters? Well, it doesn't matter now. We've got you, and Ick, and the sonic disruptor. By the time she gets back, we'll be long gone."

As Kim watched, the girls dragged Ken through the doors of Bun in the Oven. One walked over to the store computer and typed in something Kim couldn't see. The steel panic door over the fitting rooms rose up again. They bundled Ken inside and lowered it after them.

Kim needed to access that computer to open the gate. But without Ken, how was she going to do it? Her PARASITE had been removed. Homa Sidal and the ROGUE agents were on the lookout for her. It would take an army to get in there!

Kim slammed her fist down on the floor in frustration. There had to be something she could do. Her eyes wandered around GameWOW, looking for inspiration. Could she build some sort of weapon? Maybe a Taser of some kind? She had the know-how, and all the necessary parts were here, but by the time she got it done, the ROGUE agents would have disappeared.

She looked out through the broken window of the store, but there was nothing out there. In the middle of the hallway was a large display counter for Beauty Zone Cosmetics. Beyond that was an All You Can Feet shoe store, a Girls Gone Style clothing store, and an I C U camera shop.

Wait a second. . . .

An idea started to form in Kim's mind. She needed an army, right? She thought she might know just where to get one!

CHAPTER NINE

Ken's first thought upon regaining consciousness was that everything hurt: his arms, his legs, his chest, his head. His head most of all. The last time he'd hurt this bad was when he accidentally ran straight into a wall while Ippon Sensei was trying to teach him how to jump against a wall and do a backflip.

His next thought was that he was glad to regain consciousness at all. The last thing he remembered was being set on by all four ROGUE agents at the same time. At first, he'd managed to hold his own. They were still dazed from the beating he'd given them in the food court, and none wanted to be the first one to attack him. He'd used Ippon Sensei's own special fighting technique, the Poisonous Slow Loris, which combined perfect self-control with powerful elbow jabs. If Ippon Sensei had seen him, he knew she would have been proud.

But eventually the ROGUE agents had surrounded him. Two managed to grab his arms, while a third tackled his legs and held him in place. The fourth removed her high-heeled black boot to reveal two tiny Taser needles. She'd pressed them into his chest, a blast of electricity ran through his body, and that was the last thing he remembered.

As Ken came to, he realized his hands and ankles were bound together. He had been taken prisoner. He was lying on his back, being dragged by his feet.

He heard Agent 4's bubbly voice in his head.

"Remember," she had told his Stealth class, *"if you are taken prisoner, you can still gather important information. Fool your captors into thinking you are unconscious for as long as possible. They may reveal important intel. And they won't try to interrogate you!*

Learn what you can without opening your eyes. What can you hear? Smell? Feel? Look for ways to escape. If escape isn't possible, try to think of ways you can help your rescue team—because this is Spy Academy, and you will be rescued. We don't abandon our agents in the field. Will your rescue team need a distraction? Is there a place you can get to that will make it easier for them to rescue you? Think! In this situation, your mind is your best weapon."

Ken focused on keeping his breathing even and steady, as though he were still unconscious. He could feel the smooth tiled floor beneath him, and heard the sirens going off around him. That meant he was still in the mall! There was a chance they could complete their mission.

Ahead of him, the ROGUE agents were talking, but they were too quiet for Ken to hear. He strained, but could only get the occasional word or phrase—"coward," "rescue," "cute skirt."

The agents came to a halt. Ken heard a *ding!* and then felt himself being dragged across a tiny break in the floor. His head hit the edge of the gap hard, and it was all he could do not to wince.

"Doors closing," a robotic woman's voice intoned.

He was in an elevator! He must have been unconscious for only a few seconds. They were probably taking him down to Bun in the Oven, which could mean only one thing.

Homa Sidal was going to interrogate him!

Homa Sidal's interrogation techniques were legendary. There was an entire advanced seminar at Spy Academy that was taught about her. Ken had planned to take it next year. His heart started to pound. He realized he was breathing faster. He had to be careful or the ROGUEs would realize he was awake. He did his best to think about other things.

Luckily, in the small space of the elevator, Ken could hear the ROGUE agents' conversation.

"She totally ran!" said one. "What a loser."

"Yeah," said another. "Let her go get help. It won't matter. By the time they get back, there'll be nothing left here to find."

"Do you think Professor Sidal's gotten Ick to talk yet?" asked the third.

"Duh!" said the first. "Of course she has. He

might be tough, but no one can resist Professor Sidal. She'll have the sonic disruptor working by the time we get back with our new pet."

A foot hit Ken in the stomach, driving all the air out of his lungs.

"Ooph!" he said. The girls laughed.

Secretly, Ken was happy they had kicked him, because he'd almost yelled with joy when he'd heard that Ichabod was still alive and they hadn't figured out how to work the sonic disruptor yet! Kim could still take them down.

Come on, Kim, he thought.

"I'm totes stealing that dress," the fourth agent chimed in.

"The plaid one? With the blue?" asked the second.

"Ew. Gross. No, the yellow one!" responded the fourth.

For the rest of the ride, they discussed the clothes they planned to steal. It made Ken's blood boil. They were just so . . . bad!

They exited the elevator and walked down another hallway. Suddenly the texture beneath his back changed to carpet. If he had to bet, he'd guess he was back at Bun in the Oven. He heard the *click-clack* of someone typing, then the loud *KA-chung!* of a large lock opening.

That's the panic room door opening, he thought.

The agent who had been dragging him dropped his feet. Eight hands grabbed him.

"Ready?" said the second agent. "Lift!"

Ken felt himself lifted up into the air and carried into another room. This had to be Ick's secret lab.

Since the ROGUE agents had him up in the air, he figured it was probably safe to open his eyes, as none of them could see his face at this angle.

Ick's laboratory was an abandoned supply closet whose entrance had been covered over when Bun in the Oven had been built. Ick had spent the last few years scavenging things from the mall's trash to build everything he needed. His workbench was made from a giant neon letter *T*, which must have come from one of the big signs on the outside of the mall. His chairs were made from the large flowerpots that were all around the hallways, turned upside down and cushioned with scraps of rugs and bits of abandoned clothing. The whole thing was somewhere between amazingly creative and totally crazy.

As the four ROGUE agents dropped him in a corner of the lab, Ken got his first look at Ick. He was tall and skinny, with straight black hair, slightly bulging eyes, and a giant Adam's apple. He was bound hand and foot. Sitting a few feet away from him was the sonic disruptor, or so Ken guessed from the way Ick flinched anytime someone approached the strange device on the floor.

Ken stared at the sonic disruptor curiously. He was pretty sure it had started its life as one of those little robots that vacuumed the floor by themselves, with a couple of cell phones soldered on top of it and a TV satellite dish sticking out of one side. Ken wondered if something so hodgepodge could really rip a building in half. But the ROGUE agents were definitely taking it seriously, so that had to mean something.

Suddenly Homa Sidal stalked into view. She stood between Ken and Ick. Ken tried to mouth,

Help is on the way, but Ick didn't seem to see him.

"You tell me what I want to know," Homa Sidal whispered in a low, dangerous voice. "Or I'll kick this thing until it breaks—or goes off!"

"No!" screamed Ick. "Don't hurt Rumi! I'll tell you everything."

Homa Sidal laughed. "Excellent," she said. "Now, start with—"

Suddenly, a new alarm went off. It was way louder than the fire alarm. It nearly deafened Ken. It sounded like an air-raid siren. But underneath the siren, a man's voice repeated words that were music to Ken's ears.

"Intruder Alert. Intruder Alert. Intruder Alert."

Kim was on her way!

CHAPTER TEN

Homa Sidal and the four ROGUE agents all rushed to one of Ick's many computers (which were all made from fast-food-restaurant cashier terminals). Ken pulled himself upright to get a better view, hoping they were too distracted to notice him now.

"Who is it? Where are they?" screamed Homa Sidal. "You are the worst agents I have ever seen in the history of the ROGUE School. Work faster!"

One of the four ROGUE agents flinched. "I've got it," she yelled. "Mall security cameras coming up."

Her computer screen went black for a second,

then began broadcasting the live feed from each of the mall's thirty or so security cameras. They flipped by rapidly, none staying up for more than a few seconds. They showed the hallways, the escalators, the entrances, and the parking lot. They also showed Spy Academy agents, Spy Academy agents, and more Spy Academy agents! There had to be a dozen agents swarming the mall!

"Oh my God!" yelled a second agent, as she saw the images on the screen. "We're doomed."

What?! thought Ken. *How did Kim pull that off??*

Agent 4 wasn't supposed to be back at the mall for another hour, at least. All cell phone reception was jammed. Where had these agents come from?

Ken looked closely at the screen. Something about those agents looked familiar. . . .

They're all Kim! Ken realized. Kim had created a dozen disguises: There she was as a boy; there she was as a middle-aged woman; there she was as herself but with red hair and glasses! She must have grabbed the costumes, taped herself running through the mall, and then uploaded the video to the security cameras, making it look as though a full-on secret agent strike force had invaded the building.

It was brilliant!

Chaos broke loose in Ick's lab.

"Get the sonic disruptor," screamed Homa Sidal. "Pack up all the computers! We need his notes."

But the ROGUE agents were ignoring her. Two of them were frozen in terror staring at the screens. The others were grabbing anything they could get their hands on and stuffing it into matching pink teddy bear backpacks. As Ken watched, they opened the panic door and ran out of the lab.

"Get back here!" yelled Homa Sidal. "I'm failing the both of you!"

While all the ROGUEs were distracted, Ken wormed his way over to Ick, who seemed to notice him for the first time.

"You're tied up," said Ick. He sounded surprised.

"So are you," Ken replied.

"Yeah, but aren't you supposed to be rescuing me?" asked Ick. "How can you rescue me if you're a prisoner yourself?"

It was a very good question. Luckily, Ken had an idea.

"Climb under the table!" he whispered. Ick stared at him for a second, and then awkwardly complied. Ken shoved one of the planter chairs and some of the assorted tech junk in front of him. He managed to mostly hide Ick from view. It was the best he could do with his hands tied.

Another lesson Agent 4 had taught them was that sometimes, the best way of hiding one thing was to draw attention to something else.

Ken leaped to his feet.

"The game's up, Homa Sidal!" he announced. He laughed his best wicked laugh. "You fell for our plan and led us straight to Ick—whom, you might notice, I've now freed."

Homa and the remaining two ROGUE agents looked around the room wildly, but Ick was nowhere to be seen.

"I set off my Spy Academy homing beacon as soon as we entered the lab. It went right past your cell phone jamming technology. In seconds, this room is going to be crawling with Spy Academy agents. Hope you're ready to spend a good long time in jail, because that's where you're all going."

Homa Sidal stared at him for a moment. Her eyes narrowed dangerously.

"You'll never get me," she yelled. She darted forward and grabbed the sonic disruptor. "Or the sonic disruptor. The next time you see this will be when I use it to tear your headquarters down!"

There was a gasp from the junk-covered pile under which Ick was hiding. Ken covered it with a loud laugh.

"That?" Ken said. "You believe *that* is a real sonic disruptor? Look at it! It's a heap of trash. Do you really think state-of-the-art weaponry would look like a recycling pile? Ick's already run off with the real thing."

Sweat was running down the back of Ken's neck, but he tried his best to look cool, calm, and collected. If Homa didn't believe him, the sonic disruptor would fall into ROGUE hands. Even without Ick, their scientists might be able to figure out how to make it work—and how to make more of them!

"Nice try," said Homa Sidal. "But I think I'll take this toy with me, just in case."

She stepped toward the far wall of the laboratory, where Ken suddenly noticed a ladder leading up to the roof. He started to hop toward her, but before he could reach her, a brown blur came flying into the room.

BAM!

Kim slammed right into Homa Sidal, sending her tumbling to the ground. The sonic disruptor flew straight out of her hands.

"No! Rumi!" screamed Ick.

Ken watched the disruptor tumble through the air. He had to time this just perfectly. He waited . . . and waited . . . and waited. . . .

Just before the disruptor hit the floor, Ken threw himself to the ground beneath it. The disruptor landed hard on his stomach.

"Ooph!" he exclaimed.

Homa Sidal pushed Kim off of her and ran to the ladder, with the other two ROGUE agents right hind her. She scrambled up faster than Kim could ever have believed. For an old lady, she sure was quick!

"To the helicopter," Homa screamed.

"Ken!" yelled Kim.

"Rumi!" yelled Ick.

"We're fine," Ken said. "Though if you could untie me, that would be great."

The low thrum of a giant motor above them announced Homa Sidal's escape.

"Darn," said Kim, as she untied Ken's hands. "I almost had her!"

"Dude, that was awesome!" said Ken. "And that tackle was perfect—Ippon Sensei would be impressed."

"If it wasn't for you, we'd have been caught back in the food court," replied Kim. "We're definitely getting an A on this exam!"

The twins high-fived.

"Hey!" Ick's voice came from deep in the mess of the laboratory. "Somebody want to untie me?"

"Oh right, sorry!" Ken pulled Ick out and

untied him. Kim handed him the sonic disruptor, and Ick cradled it like a baby.

"So is that thing really able to rip a building in two?" she asked.

"Yes!" said Ick. "And it's very fragile. And it doesn't look like a 'recycling pile,' thank you very much! Rumi is beautiful."

He stroked the machine. Ken and Kim exchanged a long look.

Do I sound that computer crazy? Kim mouthed.

Sometimes, Ken mouthed back. Then he winked at her and smiled. He put his arm around her shoulder, and together, they walked out to the parking lot to wait for Agent 4 and M. Masque to return.

"You know," Kim said, as they sat on the curb in the busy lot, "I think I might take another Martial Arts class. It sure would have come in handy today."

"That's funny," said Ken. "Because I was thinking I might take a Tech for dummy spies class. And maybe some more Stealth classes."

And Disguise," said Kim. "I guess it really does take all the different parts to be a good spy."

They were silent for a long moment.

"Man, that's going to be a lot of school," they said in unison.

"Spy-ladies and gentle-spies of the St. Perfidious Yearling Academy," announced Principal Booker. "We are here today to honor two of our students with the highest medal that our Spy Academy has to give, the Silver Dagger."

Ken and Kim looked out on the assembled students, professors, and alumni of the academy. It was hard to believe that they were all there to celebrate the two of them.

"And to think," whispered Ken, "this is what we get for almost failing!"

Kim tried not to laugh.

"Few spies have the bravery, the intelligence, and the skill that Kim and Ken Cohen demonstrated in rescuing Ichabod Saldaña from the clutches of the evil ROGUE School."

The audience hissed at the mention of the

ROGUEs. Principal Booker waited until they grew quiet.

"In honor of these courageous students, I hereby declare the rest of the day a holiday from classes!"

The assembled crowd cheered. Ken and Kim bowed. Ippon Sensei and Dr. O pinned their Silver Dagger medals on them.

Kim took Ken's hand in hers. This year was looking up.